# Alice

## Or the Mysteries
## Book III

*by*

Edward Bulwer Lytton

Double9 BOOKS

# Alice

## Or the Mysteries

## Book III

### by Edward Bulwer Lytton



ISBN: 978-93-70429-76-5

**Published by**

**DOUBLE 9 BOOKS**
2/13-B, Ansari Road
Daryaganj, New Delhi – 110002
info@double9books.com
www.double9books.com
Tel. 011-40042856

# ABOUT THE AUTHOR

Edward George Earle Lytton Bulwer Lytton, 1st Baron Lytton, was an influential English writer and politician born on May 25, 1803, in London. A prolific author, he is best known for his novels, including The Last Days of Pompeii, Eugene Aram, and The Coming Race, which helped shape Victorian literature. His writing often explored themes of social issues, human nature, and the tension between reason and emotion. In addition to his literary career, Bulwer Lytton had a notable political life. He served as a Member of Parliament for the Whig Party from 1831 to 1841 and later as a Conservative from 1851 to 1866. He was also appointed to the House of Lords in 1866. Throughout his career, he was awarded the Chancellor's Gold Medal for his contributions to literature. He passed away on January 18, 1873, in Torquay at the age of 69. Bulwer Lytton's legacy endures through his literary works, which continue to influence modern storytelling, and his role in 19th-century politics.

# CONTENTS

Harsh things he mitigates, and pride subdues. *Ex.*
SOLON: *Eleg.*

# CHAPTER I

YOU still are what you were, sir!

. . . With most quick agility could turn
And return; make knots and undo them,
Give forked counsel.—*Volpone, or the Fox*.

B EFORE a large table, covered with parliamentary papers, sat Lumley Lord Vargrave. His complexion, though still healthy, had faded from the freshness of hue which distinguished him in youth. His features, always sharp, had grown yet more angular: his brows seemed to project more broodingly over his eyes, which, though of undiminished brightness, were sunk deep in their sockets, and had lost much of their quick restlessness. The character of his mind had begun to stamp itself on the physiognomy, especially on the mouth when in repose. It was, a face striking for acute intelligence, for concentrated energy; but there was a something written in it which said, "BEWARE!" It would have inspired any one who had mixed much amongst men with a vague suspicion and distrust.

Lumley had been always careful, though plain, in dress; but there was now a more evident attention bestowed on his person than he had ever manifested in youth,—while there was something of the Roman's celebrated foppery in the skill with which his hair was arranged on his high forehead, so as either to conceal or relieve a partial baldness at the temples. Perhaps, too, from the possession of high station, or the habit of living only amongst the great, there was a certain dignity insensibly diffused over his whole person that was not noticeable in his earlier years, when a certain *ton de garnison* was blended with his ease of manners. Yet, even now, dignity was not his prevalent characteristic; and in ordinary occasions, or mixed society, he still found a familiar frankness a more useful species of simulation. At the time we now treat of, Lord Vargrave was leaning his cheek on one hand, while the other rested idly on the papers methodically arranged before him. He appeared to have suspended his labours, and to be occupied in thought. It was, in truth, a critical period in the career of Lord Vargrave.

From the date of his accession to the peerage, the rise of Lumley Ferrers had been less rapid and progressive than he himself could have foreseen. At first, all was sunshine before him; he had contrived to make himself useful to his party; he had also made himself personally popular. To the ease and cordiality of his happy address, he added the seemingly careless candour so often mistaken for honesty; while, as there was nothing showy or brilliant in his abilities or oratory—nothing that aspired far above the pretensions of others, and aroused envy by mortifying self-love—he created but little jealousy even amongst the rivals before whom he obtained precedence. For some time, therefore, he went smoothly on, continuing to rise in the estimation of his party, and commanding a certain respect from the neutral public, by acknowledged and eminent talents in the details of business; for his quickness of penetration, and a logical habit of mind, enabled him to grapple with and generalize the minutiae of official labour or of legislative enactments with a masterly success. But as the road became clearer to his steps, his ambition became more evident and daring. Naturally dictatorial and presumptuous, his early suppleness to superiors was now exchanged for a self-willed pertinacity, which often displeased the more haughty leaders of his party, and often wounded the more vain. His pretensions were scanned with eyes more jealous and less tolerant than at first. Proud aristocrats began to recollect that a mushroom peerage was supported but by a scanty fortune; the men of more dazzling genius began to sneer at the red-tape minister as a mere official manager of details; he lost much of the personal popularity which had been one secret of his power. But what principally injured him in the eyes of his party and the public were certain ambiguous and obscure circumstances connected with a short period when himself and his associates were thrown out of office. At this time, it was noticeable that the journals of the Government that succeeded were peculiarly polite to Lord Vargrave, while they covered all his coadjutors with obloquy: and it was more than suspected that secret negotiations between himself and the new ministry were going on, when suddenly the latter broke up, and Lord Vargrave's proper party were reinstated. The vague suspicions that attached to Vargrave were somewhat strengthened in the opinion of the public by the fact that he was at first left out of the restored administration; and when subsequently, after a speech which showed that he could be mischievous if not propitiated, he was readmitted, it was precisely to the same office he had held before,—an office which did not admit him into the Cabinet. Lumley, burning with resentment, longed to decline the offer; but, alas! he was poor, and, what was worse, in debt; "his poverty, but not his will, consented." He was reinstated; but though prodigiously improved as a debater, he felt that he had not advanced as a public man. His ambition inflamed by his discontent, he had, since his return to office, strained every nerve to strengthen his position. He met the sarcasms on his poverty by greatly increasing his expenditure, and by advertising everywhere his engagement to an heiress whose fortune, great as it was, he easily contrived to magnify. As his old house in Great George Street—well fitted for the bustling commoner—was no longer suited to the official and fashionable peer, he had, on his accession to the title, exchanged that respectable residence for a large mansion in Hamilton Place; and his sober dinners were succeeded by splendid banquets. Naturally, he had no taste for such things; his mind was too nervous, and his temper too hard, to take pleasure in luxury or ostentation. But now, as ever he *acted upon a system*. Living in a country governed by the mightiest and wealthiest aristocracy in the world, which, from the first class almost to the lowest, ostentation pervades,—the very backbone and marrow of society,—he felt that to fall far short of his rivals in display was to give them an advantage which he could not compensate either by the power of his connections or the surpassing loftiness of his character and genius. Playing for a great game, and with his eyes open to all the consequences, he cared not for involving his private fortunes in a lottery in which a great prize might be drawn. To do Vargrave justice, money with him had never been an object, but a means; he was grasping, but not avaricious. If men much richer than Lord Vargrave find State distinctions very expensive, and often ruinous, it is not to be supposed that his salary, joined to so moderate a private fortune, could support the style in which he lived. His income was already deeply mortgaged, and debt accumulated upon debt. Nor had this man, so eminent for the management of public business, any of that talent which springs from *justice*, and makes its possessor a skilful manager of his own affairs. Perpetually absorbed in intrigues and schemes, he was too much engaged in cheating others on a large scale to have time to prevent being himself cheated on a small one. He never looked into bills till he was compelled to pay them; and he never calculated the amount of an expense that seemed the least necessary to his purposes. But still Lord Vargrave relied upon his marriage with the wealthy Evelyn to relieve him from all his embarrassments; and if a doubt of the realization of that vision ever occurred to him, still public life had splendid prizes. Nay, should he fail with Miss Cameron, he even thought that, by good management, he might ultimately make it worth while to his colleagues to purchase his absence with the gorgeous bribe of the Governor-Generalship of India.

As oratory is an art in which practice and the dignity of station produce marvellous improvement, so Lumley had of late made effects in the House of Lords of which he had once been judged incapable. It is true that no practice and no station can give men qualities in which they are wholly deficient; but these advantages can bring out in the best light all the qualities they *do* possess. The glow of a generous imagination, the grasp of a profound statesmanship, the enthusiasm of a noble nature,—these no practice could educe from the eloquence of Lumley Lord Vargrave, for he had them not; but bold wit, fluent and vigorous sentences, effective arrangement of parliamentary logic, readiness of retort, plausibility of manner, aided by a delivery peculiar for self-possession and ease, a clear and ringing voice (to the only fault of which, shrillness without passion, the ear of the audience had grown accustomed), and a countenance impressive from its courageous intelligence,—all these had raised the promising speaker into the matured excellence of a nervous and formidable debater. But precisely as he rose in the display of his talents, did he awaken envies and enmities hitherto dormant. And it must be added that, with all his craft and coldness, Lord Vargrave was often a very dangerous and mischievous speaker for the interests of his party. His colleagues had often cause to tremble when he rose: nay, even when the cheers of his own faction shook the old tapestried walls. A man who has no sympathy with the public must commit many and fatal indiscretions when the public, as well as his audience, is to be his judge. Lord Vargrave's utter incapacity to comprehend political morality, his contempt for all the objects of social benevolence, frequently led him into the avowal of doctrines, which, if they did not startle the men of the world whom he addressed (smoothed away, as such doctrines were, by speciousness of manner and delivery), created deep disgust in those even of his own politics who read their naked exposition in the daily papers. Never did Lord Vargrave utter one of those generous sentiments which, no matter whether propounded by Radical or Tory, sink deep into the heart of the people, and do lasting service to the cause they adorn. But no man defended an abuse, however glaring, with a more vigorous championship, or hurled defiance upon a popular demand with a more courageous scorn. In some times, when the anti-popular principle is strong; such a leader may be useful; but at the moment of which we treat he was a most equivocal auxiliary. A considerable proportion of the ministers, headed by the premier himself, a man of wise views and unimpeachable honour, had learned to view Lord Vargrave with dislike and distrust. They might have sought to get rid of him; but he was not one whom slight mortifications could induce to retire of his own accord, nor was the sarcastic and bold debater a person whose resentment and opposition could be despised. Lord Vargrave, moreover, had secured a party of his own,—a party more formidable than himself. He went largely into society; he was the special favourite of the female diplomats, whose voices at that time were powerful suffrages, and with whom, by a thousand links of gallantry and intrigue, the agreeable and courteous minister formed a close alliance. All that *salons* could do for him was done. Added to this, he was personally liked by his royal master; and the Court gave him their golden opinions; while the poorer, the corrupter, and the more bigoted portion of the ministry regarded him with avowed admiration.

In the House of Commons, too, and in the bureaucracy, he had no inconsiderable strength; for Lumley never contracted the habits of personal abruptness and discourtesy common to men in power who wish to keep applicants aloof. He was bland and conciliating to all men of ranks; his intellect and self-complacency raised him far above the petty jealousies that great men feel for rising men. Did any tyro earn the smallest distinction in parliament, no man sought his acquaintance so eagerly as Lord Vargrave; no man complimented, encouraged, "brought on" the new aspirants of his party with so hearty a good will.

Such a minister could not fail of having devoted followers among the able, the ambitious, and the vain. It must also be confessed that Lord Vargrave neglected no baser and less justifiable means to cement his power by placing it on the sure rock of self-interest. No jobbing was too gross for him. He was shamefully corrupt in the disposition of his patronage; and no rebuffs, no taunts from his official brethren, could restrain him from urging the claims of any of his creatures upon the public purse. His followers regarded this charitable selfishness as the stanchness and zeal of friendship; and the ambition of hundreds was wound up in the ambition of the unprincipled minister.

But besides the notoriety of his public corruption, Lord Vargrave was secretly suspected by some of personal dishonesty,—suspected of selling his State information to stock-jobbers, of having pecuniary interests in some of the claims he urged with so obstinate a pertinacity. And though there was not the smallest evidence of such utter abandonment of honour, though it was probably but a calumnious whisper, yet the mere suspicion of such practices served to sharpen the aversion of his enemies, and justify the disgust of his rivals.

In this position now stood Lord Vargrave: supported by interested, but able and powerful partisans; hated in the country, feared by some of those with whom he served, despised by others, looked up to by the rest. It was a situation that less daunted than delighted him; for it seemed to render necessary and excuse the habits of scheming and manoeuvre which were so genial to his crafty and plotting temper. Like an ancient Greek, his spirit loved intrigue for intrigue's sake. Had it led to no end, it would still have been sweet to him as a means. He rejoiced to surround himself with the most complicated webs and meshes; to sit in the centre of a million plots. He cared not how rash and wild some of them were. He relied on his own ingenuity, promptitude, and habitual good fortune to make every spring he handled conducive to the purpose of the machine—SELF.

His last visit to Lady Vargrave, and his conversation with Evelyn, had left on his mind much dissatisfaction and fear. In the earlier years of his intercourse with Evelyn, his good humour, gallantry, and presents had not failed to attach the child to the agreeable and liberal visitor she had been taught to regard as a relation. It was only as she grew up to womanhood, and learned to comprehend the nature of the tie between them, that she shrank from his familiarity; and then only had he learned to doubt of the fulfilment of his uncle's wish. The last visit had increased this doubt to a painful apprehension. He saw that he was not loved; he saw that it required great address, and the absence of happier rivals, to secure to him the hand of Evelyn; and he cursed the duties and the schemes which necessarily kept him from her side. He had thought of persuading Lady Vargrave to let her come to London, where he could be ever at hand; and as the season was now set in, his representations on this head would appear sensible and just. But then again this was to incur greater dangers than those he would avoid. London!—a beauty and an heiress, in her first *debut* in London! What formidable admirers would flock around her! Vargrave shuddered to think of the gay, handsome, well-dressed, seductive young *elegans*, who might seem, to a girl of seventeen, suitors far more fascinating than the middle-aged politician. This was perilous; nor was this all: Lord Vargrave knew that in London—gaudy, babbling, and remorseless London—all that he could most wish to conceal from the young lady would be dragged to day. He had been the lover, not of one, but of a dozen women, for whom he did not care three straws, but whose favour had served to strengthen him in society, or whose influence made up for his own want of hereditary political connections. The manner in which he contrived to shake off these various Ariadnes, whenever it was advisable, was not the least striking proof of his diplomatic abilities. He never left them enemies. According to his own solution of the mystery, he took care never to play the gallant with Dulcineas under a certain age. "Middle-aged women," he was wont to say, "are very little different from middle-aged men; they see things sensibly, and take things coolly." Now Evelyn could not be three weeks, perhaps three days, in London, without learning of one or the other of these *liaisons*. What an excuse, if she sought one, to break with him! Altogether, Lord Vargrave was sorely perplexed, but not despondent. Evelyn's fortune was more than ever necessary to him, and Evelyn he was resolved to obtain since to that fortune she was an indispensable appendage.

# CHAPTER II

YOU shall be Horace, and Tibullus I.—POPE.

LORD VARGRAVE was disturbed from his revery by the entrance of the Earl of Saxingham.

"You are welcome!" said Lumley, "welcome!—the very man I wished to see."

Lord Saxingham, who was scarcely altered since we met with him in the last series of this work, except that he had grown somewhat paler and thinner, and that his hair had changed from iron-gray to snow-white, threw himself in the armchair beside Lumley, and replied,—

"Vargrave, it is really unpleasant, our finding ourselves always thus controlled by our own partisans. I do not understand this new-fangled policy, this squaring of measures to please the Opposition, and throwing sops to that many-headed monster called Public Opinion. I am sure it will end most mischievously."

"I am satisfied of it," returned Lord Vargrave. "All vigour and union seem to have left us; and if they carry the ——- question against us, I know not what is to be done."

"For my part, I shall resign," said Lord Saxingham, doggedly; "it is the only alternative left to men of honour."

"You are wrong; I know another alternative."

"What is that?"

"Make a Cabinet of our own. Look ye, my dear lord; you been ill-used; your high character, your long experience, are treated with contempt. It is an affront to you—the situation you hold. You, Privy Seal!—you ought to be Premier; ay, and, if you are ruled by me, Premier you shall be yet."

Lord Saxingham coloured, and breathed hard.

"You have often hinted at this before, Lumley; but you are so partial, so friendly."

"Not at all. You saw the leading article in the ——- to-day? That will be followed up by two evening papers within five hours of this time. We have strength with the Press, with the Commons, with the Court,—only let us hold fast together. This ——- question, by which they hope to get rid of us, shall destroy them. You shall be Prime Minister before the year is over—by Heaven, you shall!—and then, I suppose, I too may be admitted to the Cabinet!"

"But how?—how, Lumley? You are too rash, too daring."

It has not been my fault hitherto,—but boldness is caution in our circumstances. If they throw us out now, I see the inevitable march of events,—we shall be out for years, perhaps for life. The Cabinet will recede more and more from our principles, our party. Now is the time for a determined stand; now can we make or mar ourselves. I will not resign; the king is with us; our strength shall be known. These haughty imbeciles shall fall into the trap they have dug for us."

Lumley spoke warmly, and with the confidence of a mind firmly assured of success. Lord Saxingham was moved; bright visions flashed across him,—the premiership, a dukedom. Yet he was old and childless, and his honours would die with the last lord of Saxingham!

"See," continued Lumley, "I have calculated our resources as accurately as an electioneering agent would cast up the list of voters. In the Press, I have secured ——- and ——-, and in the Commons we have the subtle ——-, and the vigour of ——-, and the popular name of ——-, and all the boroughs of ——-; in the Cabinet we have ——-, and at Court you know our strength. Let us choose our moment; a sudden *coup*, an interview with the king, statement of our conscientious scruples to this atrocious measure. I know the vain, stiff mind of the premier; *he* will lose temper, he will tender his resignation; to his astonishment, it will be accepted. You will be sent for; we will dissolve parliament; we will strain every nerve in the elections; we shall succeed, I know we shall. But be silent in the meanwhile, be cautious: let not a word escape you, let them think us beaten; lull suspicion asleep; let us lament our weakness, and hint, only hint at our resignation, but with assurances of continued support. I know how to blind them, if you leave it to me."

The weak mind of the old earl was as a puppet in the hands of his bold kinsman. He feared one moment, hoped another; now his ambition was flattered, now his sense of honour was alarmed. There was something in Lumley's intrigue to oust the government with which he served that had an appearance of cunning and baseness, of which Lord Saxingham, whose personal character was high, by no means approved. But Vargrave talked him over with consummate address, and when they parted, the earl carried his head two inches higher,—he was preparing himself for his rise in life.

"That is well! that is well!" said Lumley, rubbing his hands when he was left alone: "the old driveller will be my *locum tenens*, till years and renown enable me to become his successor. Meanwhile, I shall be really what he will be in name."

Here Lord Vargrave's well-fed servant, now advanced to the dignity of own gentleman and house-steward, entered the room with a letter; it had a portentous look; it was wafered, the paper was blue, the hand clerklike, there was no envelope; it bore its infernal origin on the face of it,—IT WAS A DUN'S.

Lumley opened the epistle with an impatient pshaw! The man, a silversmith (Lumley's plate was much admired!) had applied for years in vain; the amount was large, and execution was threatened! An execution!—it is a trifle to a rich man; but no trifle to one suspected of being poor, one straining at that very moment at so high an object, one to whom public opinion was so necessary, one who knew that nothing but his title, and scarcely that, saved him from the reputation of an adventurer! He must again have recourse to the money-lenders,—his small estate was long since too deeply mortgaged to afford new security. Usury, usury, again!—he knew its price, and he sighed—but what was to be done?

"It is but for a few months, a few months, and Evelyn must be mine. Saxingham has already lent me what he can; but he is embarrassed. This d---d office, what a tax it is! and the rascals say we are too well paid! I, too, who could live happy in a garret, if this purse-proud England would but allow one to exist within one's income. My fellow-trustee, the banker, my uncle's old correspondent—all, well thought of! He knows the conditions of the will; he knows that, at the worst, I must have thirty thousand pounds, if I live a few months longer. I will go to him."

# CHAPTER III

A NIMUM nunc hoc celerem, nunc dividit illuc.*—VIRGIL.

* "Now this, now that, distracts the active mind."

THE late Mr. Templeton had been a banker in a provincial town, which was the centre of great commercial and agricultural activity and enterprise. He had made the bulk of his fortune in the happy days of paper currency and war. Besides his country bank he had a considerable share in a metropolitan one of some eminence. At the time of his marriage with the present Lady Vargrave he retired altogether from business, and never returned to the place in which his wealth had been amassed. He had still kept up a familiar acquaintance with the principal and senior partner of the metropolitan bank I have referred to; for he was a man who always loved to talk about money matters with those who understood them. This gentleman, Mr. Gustavus Douce, had been named, with Lumley, joint trustee to Evelyn's fortune. They had full powers to invest it in whatever stock seemed most safe or advantageous. The trustees appeared well chosen, as one, being destined to share the fortune, would have the deepest interest in its security; and the other, from his habits and profession, would be a most excellent adviser.

Of Mr. Douce, Lord Vargrave had seen but little; they were not thrown together. But Lord Vargrave, who thought every rich man might, some time or other, become a desirable acquaintance, regularly asked him once every year to dinner; and twice in return he had dined with Mr. Douce, in one of the most splendid villas, and off some of the most splendid plate it had ever been his fortune to witness and to envy!—so that the little favour he was about to ask was but a slight return for Lord Vargrave's condescension.

He found the banker in his private sanctum, his carriage at the door; for it was just four o'clock, an hour in which Mr. Douce regularly departed to Caserta, as his aforesaid villa was somewhat affectedly styled.

Mr. Douce was a small man, a nervous man; he did not seem quite master of his own limbs: when he bowed he seemed to be making you a present of his legs; when he sat down, he twitched first on one side, then on the other, thrust his hands into his pockets, then took them out, and looked at them, as if in astonishment, then seized upon a pen, by which they were luckily provided with incessant occupation. Meanwhile, there was what might fairly be called a constant play of countenance: first he smiled, then looked grave; now raised his eyebrows, till they rose like rainbows, to the horizon of his pale, straw-coloured hair; and next darted them down, like an avalanche, over the twinkling, restless, fluttering, little blue eyes, which then became almost invisible. Mr. Douce had, in fact, all the appearance of a painfully shy man, which was the more strange, as he had the reputation of enterprise, and even audacity, in the business of his profession, and was fond of the society of the great.

"I have called on you, my dear sir," said Lord Vargrave, after the preliminary salutations, "to ask a little favour, which, if the least inconvenient, have no hesitation in refusing. You know how I am situated with regard to my ward, Miss Cameron; in a few months I hope she will be Lady Vargrave."

Mr. Douce showed three small teeth, which were all that, in the front of his mouth, fate had left him; and then, as if alarmed at the indelicacy of a smile upon such a subject, pushed back his chair, and twitched up his blotting-paper-coloured trousers.

"Yes, in a few months I hope she will be Lady Vargrave; and you know then, Mr. Douce, that I shall be in no want of money."

"I hope—that is to say, I am sure,—that—I trust that never will be the ca-ca-case with your lordship," put in Mr. Douce, with timid hesitation. Mr. Douce, in addition to his other good qualities, stammered much in the delivery of his sentences.

"You are very kind, but it is the case just at present; I have great need of a few thousand pounds upon my personal security. My estate is already a little mortgaged, and I don't wish to encumber it more; besides, the loan would be merely temporary. You know that if at the age of eighteen Miss Cameron refuses me (a supposition out of the question, but in business we must calculate on improbabilities), I claim the forfeit she incurs,—thirty thousand pounds; you remember."

"Oh, yes—that—is—upon my word—I—I don't exactly—but—your lord—l-l-l-lord-lordship knows best—I have been so—so busy—I forget the exact—hem—hem!"

"If you just turn to the will you will see it is as I say. Now, could you conveniently place a few thousands to my account, just for a short time? But I see you don't like it. Never mind, I can get it elsewhere; only, as you were my poor uncle's friend—"

"Your lord—l-l-l-lordship is quite mistaken," said Mr. Douce, with trembling agitation; "upon my word, yes, a few thou-thou-thousands—to be sure—to be sure. Your lordship's banker is—is—"

"Drummond—disagreeable people—by no means obliging. I shall certainly change to your house when my accounts are better worth keeping."

"You do me great—great honour; I will just—step—step—step out for a moment—and—and speak to Mr. Dobs;—not but what you may depend on.—Excuse me! 'Morning Chron-chron-Chronicle,' my lord!"

Mr. Douce rose, as if by galvanism, and ran out of the room, spinning round as he ran, to declare, again and again, that he would not be gone a moment.

"Good little fellow, that—very like an electrified frog!" murmured Vargrave, as he took up the "Morning Chronicle," so especially pointed out to his notice; and turning to the leading article, read a very eloquent attack on himself. Lumley was thick-skinned on such matters; he liked to be attacked,—it showed that he was up in the world.

Presently Mr. Douce returned. To Lord Vargrave's amazement and delight, he was informed that 10,000 pounds would be immediately lodged with Messrs. Drummond. His bill of promise to pay in three months—five per cent interest—was quite sufficient. Three months was a short date; but the bill could be renewed on the same terms, from quarter to quarter, till quite convenient to his lordship to pay. "Would Lord Vargrave do him the honour to dine with him at Caserta next Monday?"

Lord Vargrave tried to affect apathy at his sudden accession of ready money, but really it almost turned his head; he griped both Mr. Douce's thin, little shivering hands, and was speechless with gratitude and ecstasy. The sum, which doubled the utmost he expected, would relieve him from all his immediate embarrassments. When he recovered his voice, he thanked his dear Mr. Douce with a warmth that seemed to make the little man shrink into a nutshell; and assured him that he would dine with him every Monday in the year—if he was asked! He then longed to depart; but he thought, justly, that to go as soon as he had got what he wanted would look selfish. Accordingly, he reseated himself, and so did Mr. Douce, and the conversation turned upon politics and news; but Mr. Douce, who seemed to regard all things with a commercial eye, contrived, Vargrave hardly knew how, to veer round from the change in the French ministry to the state of the English money-market.

"It really is, indeed, my lord—I say it, I am sure, with concern, a very bad ti-ti-ti-ti-time for men in business,—indeed, for all men; such poor interest in the English fu-fun-funds, and yet speculations are so unsound. I recommended my friend Sir Giles Grimsby to—to invest some money in the American canals; a most rare res-res-respons-reponsibility, I may say, for me; I am cautious in—in recommending—but Sir Giles was an old friend,—con-con-connection, I may say; but most providentially, all turned out—that is—fell out—as I was sure it would,—thirty per cent,—and the value of the sh-sh-sh-shares doubled. But such things are very rare,—quite godsends, I may say!"

"Well, Mr. Douce, whenever I have money to lay out, I must come and consult you."

"I shall be most happy at all times to—to advise your lordship; but it is not a thing I'm very fond of. There's Miss Cameron's fortune quite l-l-locked up,—three per cents and exchequer bills; why, it might have been a mil-mil-million by this ti-ti-time, if the good old gentleman—I beg pardon—old—old nobleman, my poor dear friend, had been now alive!"

"Indeed!" said Lumley, greedily, and pricking up his ears; "he was a good manager, my uncle!"

> "None better, none better. I may say a genius for busi—hem-hem! Miss Cameron a young woman of bus-bus-business, my lord?"

"Not much of that, I fear. A million, did you say?"

"At least!—indeed, at least—money so scarce, speculation so sure in America; great people the Americans, rising people, gi-gi-giants —giants!"

"I am wasting your whole morning,—too bad in me," said Vargrave, as the clock struck five; "the Lords meet this evening,—important business; once more a thousand thanks to you; good day."

"A very good day to you, my lord; don't mention it; glad at any time to ser-ser-serve you," said Mr. Douce, fidgeting, curveting, and prancing round Lord Vargrave, as the latter walked through the outer office to the carriage.

"Not a step more; you will catch cold. Good-by—on Monday, then, seven o'clock. The House of Lords."

And Lumley threw himself back in his carriage in high spirits.

# CHAPTER IV

OUBLIE de Tullie, et brave du Senat.*
VOLTAIRE: *Brutus*, Act ii. sc. 1.

* "Forgotten by Tully and bullied by the Senate."

IN the Lords that evening the discussion was animated and prolonged,—it was the last party debate of the session. The astute Opposition did not neglect to bring prominently, though incidentally, forward the question on which it was whispered that there existed some growing difference in the Cabinet. Lord Vargrave rose late. His temper was excited by the good fortune of his day's negotiation; he felt himself of more importance than usual, as a needy man is apt to do when he has got a large sum at his banker's; moreover, he was exasperated by some personal allusions to himself, which had been delivered by a dignified old lord who dated his family from the ark, and was as rich as Croesus. Accordingly, Vargrave spoke with more than his usual vigour. His first sentences were welcomed with loud cheers; he warmed, he grew vehement, he uttered the most positive and unalterable sentiments upon the question alluded to, he greatly transgressed the discretion which the heads of his party were desirous to maintain,—instead of conciliating without compromising, he irritated, galled, *and* compromised. The angry cheers of the opposite party were loudly re-echoed by the cheers of the more hot-headed on his own side. The premier and some of his colleagues observed, however, a moody silence. The premier once took a note, and then reseated himself, and drew his hat more closely over his brows. It was an ominous sign for Lumley; but he was looking the Opposition in the face, and did not observe it. He sat down in triumph; he had made a most effective and a most mischievous speech,—a combination extremely common. The leader of the Opposition replied to him with bitter calmness; and when citing some of his sharp sentences, he turned to the premier, and asked, "Are these opinions those also of the noble lord? I call for a reply,—I have a right to demand a reply," Lumley was startled to hear the tone in which his chief uttered the comprehensive and significant "*Hear, hear*!"

At midnight the premier wound up the debate; his speech was short, and characterized by moderation. He came to the question put to him. The House was hushed,—you might have heard a pin drop; the Commoners behind the throne pressed forward with anxiety and eagerness on their countenances.

"I am called upon," said the minister, "to declare if those sentiments, uttered by my noble friend, are mine also, as the chief adviser of the Crown. My lords, in the heat of debate every word is not to be scrupulously weighed, and rigidly interpreted." ("Hear, hear," ironically from the Opposition, approvingly from the Treasury benches.) "My noble friend will doubtless be anxious to explain what he intended to say. I hope, nay, I doubt not, that his explanation will be satisfactory to the noble lord, to the House, and to the country; but since I am called upon for a distinct reply to a distinct interrogatory, I will say at once, that if those sentiments be rightly interpreted by the noble lord who spoke last, those sentiments are not mine, and will never animate the conduct of any cabinet of which I am a member." (Long-continued cheering from the Opposition.) "At the same time, I am convinced that my noble friend's meaning has not been rightly construed; and till I hear from himself to the contrary, I will venture to state what I think he designed to convey to your lordships." Here the premier, with a tact that nobody could be duped by, but every one could admire, stripped Lord Vargrave's unlucky sentences of every syllable that could give offence to any one; and left the pointed epigrams and vehement denunciations a most harmless arrangement of commonplace.

The House was much excited; there was a call for Lord Vargrave, and Lord Vargrave promptly rose. It was one of those dilemmas out of which Lumley was just the man to extricate himself with address. There was so much manly frankness in his manner, there was so much crafty subtlety in his mind! He complained, with proud and honest bitterness, of the construction that had been forced upon his words by the Opposition. "If," he added (and no man knew better the rhetorical effect of the _tu quoque form of argument),—"if every sentence uttered by the noble lord opposite in his zeal for liberty had, in days now gone by, been construed with equal rigour, or perverted with equal ingenuity, that noble lord had long since been prosecuted as an incendiary, perhaps executed as a traitor!" Vehement cheers from the ministerial benches; cries of "Order!" from the Opposition. A military lord rose to order, and appealed to the Woolsack.

Lumley sat down as if chafed at the interruption; he had produced the effect he had desired,—he had changed the public question at issue into a private quarrel; a new excitement was created; dust was thrown into the eyes of the House. Several speakers rose to accommodate matters; and after half-an-hour of public time had been properly wasted, the noble lord on the one side and the noble lord on the other duly explained, paid each other the highest possible compliments, and Lumley was left to conclude his vindication, which now seemed a comparatively flat matter after the late explosion. He completed his task so as to satisfy, apparently, all parties—for all parties were now tired of the thing, and wanted to go to bed. But the next morning there were whispers about the town, articles in the different papers, evidently by authority, rejoicings among the Opposition, and a general feeling that though the Government might keep together that session, its dissensions would break out before the next meeting of parliament.

As Lumley was wrapping himself in his cloak after this stormy debate, the Marquess of Raby—a peer of large possessions, and one who entirely agreed with Lumley's views—came up to him, and proposed that they should go home together in Lord Raby's carriage. Vargrave willingly consented, and dismissed his own servants.

"You did that admirably, my dear Vargrave!" said Lord Raby, when they were seated in the carriage. "I quite coincide in all your sentiments; I declare my blood boiled when I heard ——- [the premier] appear half inclined to throw you over. Your hit upon ——- was first-rate,—he will not get over it for a month; and you extricated yourself well."

"I am glad you approve my conduct,—it comforts me," said Vargrave, feelingly; "at the same time I see all the consequences; but I can brave all for the sake of character and conscience."

"I feel just as you do!" replied Lord Raby, with some warmth; "and if I thought that ——- meant to yield to this question, I should certainly oppose his administration."

Vargrave shook his head, and held his tongue, which gave Lord Raby a high idea of his discretion.

After a few more observations on political matters, Lord Raby invited Lumley to pay him a visit at his country-seat.

"I am going to Knaresdean next Monday; you know we have races in the park, and really they are sometimes good sport; at all events, it is a very pretty sight. There will be nothing in the Lords now,—the recess is just at hand; and if you can spare the time, Lady Raby and myself will be delighted to see you."

"You may be sure, my dear lord, I cannot refuse your invitation; indeed, I intended to visit your county next week. You know, perhaps, a Mr. Merton."

"Charles Merton?—to be sure; most respectable man, capital fellow, the best parson in the county,—no cant, but thoroughly orthodox; he certainly keeps in his brother, who, though a very active member, is what I call a waverer on certain questions. Have you known Merton long?"

"I don't know him at all as yet; my acquaintance is with his wife and daughter,—a very fine girl, by the by. My ward, Miss Cameron, is staying with them."

"Miss Cameron! Cameron—ah, I understand. I think I have heard that— But gossip does not always tell the truth!"

Lumley smiled significantly, and the carriage now stopped at his door.

"Perhaps you will take a seat in our carriage on Monday?" said Lord Raby.

"Monday? Unhappily I am engaged; but on Tuesday your lordship may expect me."

"Very well; the races begin on Wednesday: we shall have a full house. Good-night."

# CHAPTER V

H OMUNCULI quanti sunt, cum recogito.*—PLAUTUS.

* "When I reflect, how great your little men are in their own consideration!"

IT is obvious that for many reasons we must be brief upon the political intrigue in which the scheming spirit of Lord Vargrave was employed. It would, indeed, be scarcely possible to preserve the necessary medium between too plain a revelation and too complex a disguise. It suffices, therefore, very shortly to repeat what the reader has already gathered from what has gone before; namely, that the question at issue was one which has happened often enough in all governments,—one on which the Cabinet was divided, and in which the weaker party was endeavouring to out-trick the stronger.

The malcontents, foreseeing that sooner or later the head of the gathering must break, were again divided among themselves whether to resign, or to stay in and strive to force a resignation on their dissentient colleagues. The richer and the more honest were for the former course; the poorer and the more dependent for the latter. We have seen that the latter policy was that espoused and recommended by Vargrave, who, though not in the Cabinet, always contrived somehow or other to worm out its secrets. At the same time he by no means rejected the other string to his bow. If it were possible so to arrange and to strengthen his faction, that, by the *coup d'etat* of a sudden resignation in a formidable body, the whole Government might be broken up, and a new one formed from among the resignees, it would obviously be the best plan. But then Lord Vargrave was doubtful of his own strength, and fearful to play into the hands of his colleagues, who might be able to stand even better without himself and his allies, and by conciliating the Opposition take a step onward in political movement,—which might leave Vargrave placeless and powerless for years to come.

He repented his own rashness in the recent debate, which was, indeed, a premature boldness that had sprung out of momentary excitement—for the craftiest orator must be indiscreet sometimes. He spent the next few days in alternately seeking to explain away to one party, and to sound, unite, and consolidate the other. His attempts in the one quarter were received by the premier with the cold politeness of an offended but careful statesman, who believed just as much as he chose, and preferred taking his own opportunity for a breach with a subordinate to risking any imprudence by the gratification of resentment. In the last quarter, the penetrating adventurer saw that his ground was more insecure than he had anticipated. He perceived in dismay and secret rage that many of those most loud in his favour while he was with the Government would desert him the soonest if thrown out. Liked as a subordinate minister, he was viewed with very different eyes the moment it was a question whether, instead of cheering his sentiments, men should trust themselves to his guidance. Some did not wish to displease the Government; others did not seek to weaken but to correct them. One of his stanchest allies in the Commons was a candidate for a peerage; another suddenly remembered that he was second cousin to the premier. Some laughed at the idea of a puppet premier in Lord Saxingham; others insinuated to Vargrave that he himself was not precisely of that standing in the country which would command respect to a new party, of which, if not the head, he would be the mouthpiece. For themselves they knew, admired, and trusted him; but those d—-d country gentlemen—and the dull public!

Alarmed, wearied, and disgusted, the schemer saw himself reduced to submission, for the present at least; and more than ever he felt the necessity of Evelyn's fortune to fall back upon, if the chance of the cards should rob him of his salary. He was glad to escape for a breathing-while from the vexations and harassments that beset him, and looked forward with the eager interest of a sanguine and elastic mind—always escaping from one scheme to another—to his excursion into B—-shire.

At the villa of Mr. Douce, Lord Vargrave met a young nobleman who had just succeeded to a property not only large and unencumbered, but of a nature to give him importance in the eyes of politicians. Situated in a very small county, the estates of Lord Doltimore secured to his nomination at least one of the representatives, while a little village at the back of his pleasure-grounds constituted a borough, and returned two members to parliament. Lord Doltimore, just returned from the Continent, had not even taken his seat in the Lords; and though his family connections, such as they were—and they were not very high, and by no means in the fashion—were ministerial, his own opinions were as yet unrevealed.

To this young nobleman Lord Vargrave was singularly attentive. He was well formed to attract men younger than himself, and he eminently succeeded in his designs upon Lord Doltimore's affection.

His lordship was a small, pale man, with a very limited share of understanding, supercilious in manner, elaborate in dress, not ill-natured *au fond*, and with much of the English gentleman in his disposition,—that is, he was honourable in his ideas and actions, whenever his natural dulness and neglected education enabled him clearly to perceive (through the mid of prejudices, the delusions of others, and the false lights of the dissipat society in which he had lived) what was right and what wrong. But h leading characteristics were vanity and conceit. He had lived much wi younger sons, cleverer than himself, who borrowed his money, sold hi their horses, and won from him at cards. In return they gave him all th species of flattery which young men *can* give with so hearty an appearan of cordial admiration. "You certainly have the best horses in Paris. You a really a devilish good fellow, Doltimore. Oh, do you know, Doltimore, wh little Desire says of you? You have certainly turned the girl's head."

This sort of adulation from one sex was not corrected by any gre acerbity from the other. Lord Doltimore at the age of twenty-two was very good *parti*; and, whatever his other deficiencies, he had sense enou to perceive that he received much greater attention—whether from ope dancers in search of a friend, or virtuous young ladies in search of husband—than any of the companions, good-looking though many of the were, with whom he had habitually lived.

"You will not long remain in town now the season is over?" sa Vargrave, as after dinner he found himself, by the departure of the ladi next to Lord Doltimore.

"No, indeed; even in the season I don't much like London. Paris h rather spoiled me for any other place."

"Paris is certainly very charming; the ease of French life has a fascinati that our formal ostentation wants. Nevertheless, to a man like you, Lond must have many attractions."

"Why, I have a good many friends here; but still, after Ascot, it rath bores me."

"Have you any horses on the turf?"

"Not yet; but Legard (you know Legard, perhaps,—a very good fello is anxious that I should try my luck. I was very fortunate in the races Paris—you know we have established racing there. The French take to quite naturally."

"Ah, indeed! It is so long since I have been in Paris—most exciti amusement! *A propos* of races, I am going down to Lord Raby's to-morro I think I saw in one of the morning papers that you had very largely back a horse entered at Knaresdean."

"Yes, Thunderer—I think of buying Thunderer. Legard—Colo Legard (he was in the Guards, but he sold out)—is a good judge, a recommends the purchase. How very odd that you too should be going Knaresdean!"

"Odd, indeed, but most lucky! We can go together, if you are not better engaged."

Lord Doltimore coloured and hesitated. On the one hand he was a little afraid of being alone with so clever a man; on the other hand, it was an honour,—it was something for him to talk of to Legard. Nevertheless, the shyness got the better of the vanity. He excused himself; he feared he was engaged to take down Legard.

Lumley smiled, and changed the conversation; and so agreeable did he make himself, that when the party broke up, and Lumley had just shaken hands with his host, Doltimore came to him, and said in a little confusion,—

"I think I can put off Legard—if—if you—"

"That's delightful! What time shall we start?—need not get down much before dinner—one o'clock?"

"Oh, yes! not too long before dinner; one o'clock will be a little too early."

"Two then. Where are you staying?"

"At Fenton's."

"I will call for you. Good-night! I long to see Thunderer!"

# CHAPTER VI

LA sante de l'ame n'est pas plus assuree que celle du corps; et quoique l'on paraisse eloigne des passions, on n'est pas moins en danger de s'y laisser emporter que de tomber malade quand on se porte bien.*—LA ROCHEFOUCAULD.

* "The health of the soul is not more sure than that of the body; and although we may appear free from passions, there is not the less danger of their attack than of falling sick at the moment we are well."

IN spite of the efforts of Maltravers to shun all occasions of meeting Evelyn, they were necessarily sometimes thrown together in the round of provincial hospitalities; and certainly, if either Mr. Merton or Caroline (the shrewder observer of the two) had ever formed any suspicion that Evelyn had made a conquest of Maltravers, his manner at such times effectually removed it.

Maltravers was a man to feel deeply, but no longer a boy to yield to every tempting impulse. I have said that FORTITUDE was his favourite virtue, but fortitude is the virtue of great and rare occasions; there was another, equally hard-favoured and unshowy, which he took as the staple of active and every-day duties, and that virtue was JUSTICE. Now, in earlier life, he had been enamoured of the conventional Florimel that we call HONOUR,—a shifting and shadowy phantom, that is but the reflex of the opinion of the time and clime. But justice has in it something permanent and solid; and out of justice arises the real not the false honour.

"Honour!" said Maltravers,—"honour is to justice as the flower to the plant,—its efflorescence, its bloom, its consummation! But honour that does not spring from justice is but a piece of painted rag, an artificial rose, which the men-milliners of society would palm upon us as more natural than the true."

This principle of justice Maltravers sought to carry out in all things—not, perhaps, with constant success; for what practice can always embody theory?—but still, at least his endeavour at success was constant. This, perhaps, it was which had ever kept him from the excesses to which exuberant and liberal natures are prone, from the extravagances of pseudo-genius.

"No man, for instance," he was wont to say, "can be embarrassed in his own circumstances, and not cause embarrassment to others. Without economy, who can be just? And what are charity, generosity, but the poetry and the beauty of justice?"

No man ever asked Maltravers twice for a just debt; and no man ever once asked him to fulfil a promise. You felt that, come what would, you might rely upon his word. To him might have been applied the witty eulogium passed by Johnson upon a certain nobleman: "If he had promised you an acorn, and the acorn season failed in England, he would have sent to Norway for one!"

It was not, therefore, the mere Norman and chivalrous spirit of honour, which he had worshipped in youth as a part of the Beautiful and the Becoming, but which in youth had yielded to temptation, as a *sentiment* ever must yield to a passion, but it was the more hard, stubborn, and reflective *principle,* which was the later growth of deeper and nobler wisdom, that regulated the conduct of Maltravers in this crisis of his life. Certain it is, that he had never but once loved as he loved Evelyn; and yet that he never yielded so little to the passion.

"If engaged to another," thought he, "that engagement it is not for a third person to attempt to dissolve. I am the last to form a right judgment of the strength or weakness of the bonds which unite her to Vargrave, for my emotions would prejudice me despite myself. I may fancy that her betrothed is not worthy of her,—but that is for her to decide. While the bond lasts, who can be justified in tempting her to break it?"

Agreeably to these notions, which the world may, perhaps, consider overstrained, whenever Maltravers met Evelyn, he intrenched himself in a rigid and almost a chilling formality. How difficult this was with one so simple and ingenuous! Poor Evelyn! she thought she had offended him; she longed to ask him her offence,—perhaps, in her desire to rouse his genius into exertion, she had touched some secret sore, some latent wound of the memory? She recalled all their conversations again and again. Ah, why could they not be renewed? Upon her fancy and her thoughts Maltravers had made an impression not to be obliterated. She wrote more frequently than ever to Lady Vargrave, and the name of Maltravers was found in every page of her correspondence.

One evening, at the house of a neighbour, Miss Cameron (with the Mertons) entered the room almost in the same instant as Maltravers. The party was small, and so few had yet arrived that it was impossible for

Maltravers, without marked rudeness, to avoid his friends from the rectory; and Mrs. Merton, placing herself next to Evelyn, graciously motioned to Maltravers to occupy the third vacant seat on the sofa, of which she filled the centre.

"We grudge all your improvements, Mr. Maltravers, since they cost us your society. But we know that our dull circle must seem tame to one who has seen so much. However, we expect to offer you an inducement soon in Lord Vargrave. What a lively, agreeable person he is!"

Maltravers raised his eyes to Evelyn, calmly and penetratingly, at the latter part of this speech. He observed that she turned pale, and sighed involuntarily.

"He had great spirits when I knew him," said he; "and he had then less cause to make him happy."

Mrs. Merton smiled, and turned rather pointedly towards Evelyn.

Maltravers continued, "I never met the late lord. He had none of the vivacity of his nephew, I believe."

"I have heard that he was very severe," said Mrs. Merton, lifting her glass towards a party that had just entered.

"Severe!" exclaimed Evelyn. "Ah, if you could have known him! the kindest, the most indulgent—no one ever loved me as he did." She paused, for she felt her lip quiver.

"I beg your pardon, my dear," said Mrs. Merton, coolly. Mrs. Merton had no idea of the pain inflicted by *treading upon a feeling*. Maltravers was touched, and Mrs. Merton went on. "No wonder he was kind to you, Evelyn,—a brute would be that; but he was generally considered a stern man."

"I never saw a stern look, I never heard a harsh word; nay, I do not remember that he ever even used the word 'command,'" said Evelyn, almost angrily.

Mrs. Merton was about to reply, when suddenly seeing a lady whose little girl had been ill of the measles, her motherly thoughts flowed into a new channel, and she fluttered away in that sympathy which unites all the heads of a growing family. Evelyn and Maltravers were left alone.

"You do not remember your father, I believe?" said Maltravers.

"No father but Lord Vargrave; while he lived, I never knew the loss of one."

"Does your mother resemble you?"

"Ah, I wish I could think so; it is the sweetest countenance!"

"Have you no picture of her?"

"None; she would never consent to sit."

"Your father was a Cameron; I have known some of that name."

"No relation of ours: my mother says we have none living."

"And have we no chance of seeing Lady Vargrave in B— —-shire?"

"She never leaves home; but I hope to return soon to Brook-Green."

Maltravers sighed, and the conversation took a new turn.

"I have to thank you for the books you so kindly sent; I ought to have returned them ere this," said Evelyn.

"I have no use for them. Poetry has lost its charm for me,—especially that species of poetry which unites with the method and symmetry something of the coldness of Art. How did you like Alfieri?"

"His language is a kind of Spartan French," answered Evelyn, in one of those happy expressions which every now and then showed the quickness of her natural talent.

"Yes," said Maltravers, smiling, "the criticism is acute. Poor Alfieri! in his wild life and his stormy passions he threw out all the redundance of his genius; and his poetry is but the representative of his thoughts, not his emotions. Happier the man of genius who lives upon his reason, and wastes feeling only on his verse!"

"You do not think that we *waste* feeling upon human beings?" said Evelyn, with a pretty laugh.

"Ask me that question when you have reached my years, and can look upon fields on which you have lavished your warmest hopes, your noblest aspirations, your tenderest affections, and see the soil all profitless and barren. 'Set not your heart on the things of earth,' saith the Preacher."

Evelyn was affected by the tone, the words, and the melancholy countenance of the speaker. "You, of all men, ought not to think thus," said she, with a sweet eagerness; "you who have done so much to awaken and to soften the heart in others; you—who—" she stopped short, and added, more gravely. "Ah, Mr. Maltravers, I cannot reason with you, but I can hope you will refute your own philosophy."

"Were your wish fulfilled," answered Maltravers, almost with sternness, and with an expression of great pain in his compressed lips, "I should have to thank you for much misery." He rose abruptly, and turned away.

"How have I offended him?" thought Evelyn, sorrowfully; "I never speak but to wound him. What *have* I done?"

She could have wished, in her simple kindness, to follow him, and make peace; but he was now in a coterie of strangers; and shortly afterwards he left the room, and she did not see him again for weeks.

# CHAPTER VII

N IHIL est aliud magnum quam multa minuta.*—
VETUS. AUCTOR.

* "There is nothing so great as the collection of the minute."

AN anxious event disturbed the smooth current of cheerful life at Merton Rectory. One morning when Evelyn came down, she missed little Sophy, who had contrived to establish for herself the undisputed privilege of a stool beside Miss Cameron at breakfast. Mrs. Merton appeared with a graver face than usual. Sophy was unwell, was feverish; the scarlet fever had been in the neighbourhood. Mrs. Merton was very uneasy.

"It is the more unlucky, Caroline," added the mother, turning to Miss Merton, "because to-morrow, you know, we were to have spent a few days at Knaresdean to see the races. If poor Sophy does not get better, I fear you and Miss Cameron must go without me. I can send to Mrs. Hare to be your chaperon; she would be delighted."

"Poor Sophy!" said Caroline; "I am very sorry to hear she is unwell; but I think Taylor would take great care of her; you surely need not stay, unless she is much worse."

Mrs. Merton, who, tame as she seemed, was a fond and attentive mother, shook her head and said nothing; but Sophy was much worse before noon. The doctor was sent for, and pronounced it to be the scarlet fever.

It was now necessary to guard against the infection. Caroline had had the complaint, and she willingly shared in her mother's watch of love for two or three hours. Mrs. Merton gave up the party. Mrs. Hare (the wife of a rich squire in the neighbourhood) was written to, and that lady willingly agreed to take charge of Caroline and her friend.

Sophy had been left asleep. When Mrs. Merton returned to her bed, she found Evelyn quietly stationed there. This alarmed her, for Evelyn had never had the scarlet fever, and had been forbidden the sick-room. But poor little Sophy had waked and querulously asked for her dear Evy; and Evy, who had been hovering round the room, heard the inquiry from the garrulous nurse, and come in she would; and the child gazed at her so beseechingly, when Mrs. Merton entered, and said so piteously, "Don't take

Evy away," that Evelyn stoutly declared that she was not the least afraid of infection, and stay she must. Nay, her share in the nursing would be the more necessary since Caroline was to go to Knaresdean the next day.

"But you go too, my dear Miss Cameron?"

"Indeed I could not. I don't care for races, I never wished to go, I would much sooner have stayed; and I am sure Sophy will not get well without me,—will you, dear?"

"Oh, yes, yes; if I'm to keep you from the nice races, I should be worse if I thought that."

"But I don't like the nice races, Sophy, as your sister Carry does; she must go,—they can't do without her; but nobody knows me, so I shall not be missed."

"I can't hear of such a thing," said Mrs. Merton, with tears in her eyes; and Evelyn said no more then. But the next morning Sophy was still worse, and the mother was too anxious and too sad to think more of ceremony and politeness, so Evelyn stayed.

A momentary pang shot across Evelyn's breast when all was settled; but she suppressed the sigh which accompanied the thought that she had lost the only opportunity she might have for weeks of seeing Maltravers. To that chance she had indeed looked forward with interest and timid pleasure. The chance was lost; but why should it vex her,—what was he to her?

Caroline's heart smote her, as she came into the room in her lilac bonnet and new dress; and little Sophy, turning on her eyes which, though languid, still expressed a child's pleasure at the sight of finery, exclaimed, "How nice and pretty you look, Carry! Do take Evy with you,—Evy looks pretty too!"

Caroline kissed the child in silence, and paused irresolute; glanced at her dress, and then at Evelyn, who smiled on her without a thought of envy; and she had half a mind to stay too, when her mother entered with a letter from Lord Vargrave. It was short: he should be at the Knaresdean races, hoped to meet them there, and accompany them home. This information re-decided Caroline, while it rewarded Evelyn. In a few minutes more, Mrs. Hare arrived; and Caroline, glad to escape, perhaps, her own compunction, hurried into the carriage, with a hasty "God bless you all! Don't fret—I'm sure she will be well to-morrow; and mind, Evelyn, you don't catch the fever!" Mr. Merton looked grave and sighed, as he handed her into the carriage; but when, seated there, she turned round and kissed her hand at him, she looked so handsome and distinguished, that a sentiment of paternal pride smoothed down his vexation at her want of feeling. He himself gave up the visit; but a little time after, when Sophy fell into a tranquil sleep, he thought he might venture to canter across the country to the race-ground, and return to dinner.

Days—nay, a whole week passed, the races were over, but Caroline had not returned. Meanwhile, Sophy's fever left her; she could quit her bed, her room; she could come downstairs now, and the family was happy. It is astonishing how the least ailment in those little things stops the wheels of domestic life! Evelyn fortunately had not caught the fever: she was pale, and somewhat reduced by fatigue and confinement; but she was amply repaid by the mother's swimming look of quiet gratitude, the father's pressure of the hand, Sophy's recovery, and her own good heart. They had heard twice from Caroline, putting off her return: Lady Raby was so kind, she could not get away till the party broke up; she was so glad to hear such an account of Sophy.

Lord Vargrave had not yet arrived at the rectory to stay; but he had twice ridden over, and remained there some hours. He exerted himself to the utmost to please Evelyn; and she—who, deceived by his manners, and influenced by the recollections of long and familiar acquaintance, was blinded to his real character—reproached herself more bitterly than ever for her repugnance to his suit and her ungrateful hesitation to obey the wishes of her stepfather.

To the Mertons, Lumley spoke with good-natured praise of Caroline; she was so much admired; she was the beauty at Knaresdean. A certain young friend of his, Lord Doltimore, was evidently smitten. The parents thought much over the ideas conjured up by that last sentence.

One morning, the garrulous Mrs. Hare, the gossip of the neighbourhood, called at the rectory; she had returned, two days before, from Knaresdean; and she, too, had her tale to tell of Caroline's conquests.

"I assure you, my dear Mrs. Merton, if we had not all known that his heart was pre-occupied, we should have thought that Lord Vargrave was her warmest admirer. Most charming man, Lord Vargrave! but as for Lord Doltimore, it was quite a flirtation. Excuse *me*: no scandal, you know, ha, ha! a fine young man, but stiff and reserved,—not the fascination of Lord Vargrave."

"Does Lord Raby return to town, or is he now at Knaresdean for the autumn?"

> "He goes on Friday, I believe: very few of the guests are left now. Lady A. and Lord B., and Lord Vargrave and your daughter, and Mr. Legard and Lord Doltimore, and Mrs. and the Misses Cipher; all the rest went the same day I did."

"Indeed!" said Mrs. Merton, in some surprise.

"Ah, I read your thoughts: you wonder that Miss Caroline has not come back,—is not that it? But perhaps Lord Doltimore—ha, ha!—no scandal now—do excuse *me*!"

"Was Mr. Maltravers at Knaresdean?" asked Mrs. Merton, anxious to change the subject, and unprepared with any other question. Evelyn was cutting out a paper horse for Sophy, who—all her high spirits flown—was lying on the sofa, and wistfully following her fairy fingers. "Naughty Evy, you have cut off the horse's head!"

"Mr. Maltravers? No, I think not; no, he was not there. Lord Raby asked him pointedly to come, and was, I know, much disappointed that he did not. But *a propos* of Mr. Maltravers: I met him not a quarter of an hour ago, this morning, as I was coming to you. You know we have leave to come through his park, and as I was in the park at the time, I stopped the carriage to speak to him. I told him that I was coming here, and that you had had the scarlet fever in the house, which was the reason you had not gone to the races; and he turned quite pale, and seemed so alarmed. I said we were all afraid that Miss Cameron should catch it; and, excuse me—ah, ah!—no scandal, I hope—but—"

"Mr. Maltravers," said the butler, throwing open the door. Maltravers entered with a quick and even a hurried step. He stopped short when he saw Evelyn; and his whole countenance was instantly lightened up by a joyous expression, which as suddenly died away.

"This is kind, indeed," said Mrs. Merton; "it is so long since we have seen you."

"I have been very much occupied," muttered Maltravers, almost inaudibly, and seated himself next Evelyn. "I only just heard—that—that you had sickness in the house. Miss Cameron, you look pale—you—you have not suffered, I hope?"

"No, I am quite well," said Evelyn, with a smile; and she felt happy that her friend was kind to her once more.

"It's only me, Mr. Ernest," said Sophy; "you have forgot me."

Maltravers hastened to vindicate himself from the charge, and Sophy and he were soon made excellent friends again. Mrs. Hare, whom surprise at this sudden meeting had hitherto silenced, and who longed to shape into elegant periphrasis the common adage, "Talk of," etc., now once more opened her budget. She tattled on, first to one, then to the other, then to all, till she had tattled herself out of breath; and then the orthodox half-hour was expired, and the bell was rung, and the carriage ordered, and Mrs. Hare rose to depart.

"Do just come to the door, Mrs. Merton," said she, "and look at my pony-phaeton, it is so pretty; Lady Raby admires it so much; you ought to have just such another." As she spoke, she favoured Mrs. Merton with a significant glance, that said, as plainly as glance could say, "I have something to communicate." Mrs. Merton took the hint, and followed t good lady out of the room.

"Do you know, my dear Mrs. Merton," said Mrs. Hare, in a whisp when they were safe in the billiard-room, that interposed between t apartment they had left and the hall; "do you know whether Lord Vargra and Mr. Maltravers are very good friends?"

"No, indeed; why do you ask?"

"Oh, because when I was speaking to Lord Vargrave about him, shook his head; and really I don't remember what his lordship said, l he seemed to speak as if there was a little soreness. And then he inqui very anxiously if Mr. Maltravers was much at the rectory; and look discomposed when he found you were such near neighbours. You'll exc me, you know—ha, ha! but we're such old friends!—and if Lord Vargrav coming to stay here, it might be unpleasant to meet—you'll excuse *me*. I tc the liberty to tell him he need not be jealous of Mr. Maltravers—ha, ha!— a marrying man at all. But I did think Miss Caroline was the attractio you'll excuse me—no scandal—ha, ha! But, after all, Lord Doltimore m be the man. Well, good morning, I thought I'd just give you this hint. Is the phaeton pretty? Kind compliments to Mr. Merton."

And the lady drove off.

During this confabulation, Maltravers and Evelyn were left alone w Sophy. Maltravers had continued to lean over the child, and appea listening to her prattle; while Evelyn, having risen to shake hands with M Hare, did not reseat herself, but went to the window, and busied her with a flower-stand in the recess.

"Oh, very fine, Mr. Ernest," said Sophy (always pronouncing t proper name as if it ended in *th*), "you care very much for us to stay awa long,—don't he, Evy? I've a great mind not to speak to you, sir, that I hav

"That would be too heavy a punishment, Miss Sophy, only, luckil would punish yourself; you could not live without talking—talk—talk talk!"

"But I might never have talked more, Mr. Ernest, if Mamma and pr Evy had not been so kind to me;" and the child shook her head mournfu as if she had *pitie de soi-meme*. "But you won't stay away so long again, you? Sophy play to-morrow; come to-morrow, and swing Sophy; no swinging since you've been gone."

While Sophy spoke Evelyn turned half round, as if to hear Maltra answer; he hesitated, and Evelyn spoke.

"You must not tease Mr. Maltravers so; Mr. Maltravers has too muc do to come to us."

Now this was a very pettish speech in Evelyn, and her cheek glowed while she spoke; but an arch, provoking smile was on her lips.

"It can be a privation only to me, Miss Cameron," said Maltravers, rising, and attempting in vain to resist the impulse that drew him towards the window. The reproach in her tone and words at once pained and delighted him; and then this scene, the suffering child, brought back to him his first interview with Evelyn herself. He forgot, for the moment, the lapse of time, the new ties she had formed, his own resolutions.

"That is a bad compliment to us," answered Evelyn, ingenuously; "do you think we are so little worthy your society as not to value it? But, perhaps" (she added, sinking her voice) "perhaps you have been offended—perhaps I—I—said—something that—that hurt you!"

"You!" repeated Maltravers, with emotion.

Sophy, who had been attentively listening, here put in, "Shake hands and make it up with Evy—you've been quarrelling, naughty Ernest!"

Evelyn laughed, and tossed back her sunny ringlets. "I think Sophy is right," said she, with enchanting simplicity; "let us make it up," and she held out her hand to Maltravers.

Maltravers pressed the fair hand to his lips. "Alas!" said he, affected with various feelings which gave a tremor to his deep voice, "your only fault is that your society makes me discontented with my solitary home; and as solitude must be my fate in life, I seek to inure myself to it betimes."

Here—whether opportunely or not, it is for the reader to decide—Mrs. Merton returned to the room.

She apologized for her absence, talked of Mrs. Hare and the little Master Hares,—fine boys, but noisy; and then she asked Maltravers if he had seen Lord Vargrave since his lordship had been in the county. Maltravers replied, with coldness, that he had not had that honour: that Vargrave had called on him in his way from the rectory the other day, but that he was from home, and that he had not seen him for some years.

"He is a person of most prepossessing manners," said Mrs. Merton.

"Certainly,—most prepossessing."

"And very clever."

"He has great talents."

"He seems most amiable."

Maltravers bowed, and glanced towards Evelyn, whose face, however, was turned from him.

The turn the conversation had taken was painful to the visitor, and he rose to depart.

"Perhaps," said Mrs. Merton, "you will meet Lord Vargrave at dinner to-morrow; he will stay with us a few days,—as long as he can be spared."

Maltravers meet Lord Vargrave! the happy Vargrave, the betrothed to Evelyn! Maltravers witness the familiar rights, the enchanting privileges, accorded to another! and that other one whom he could not believe worthy of Evelyn! He writhed at the picture the invitation conjured up.

> "You are very kind, my dear Mrs. Merton, but I expect a visitor at Burleigh,—an old and dear friend, Mr. Cleveland."

"Mr. Cleveland!—we shall be delighted to see him too. We knew him many years ago, during your minority, when he used to visit Burleigh two or three times a year."

"He is changed since then; he is often an invalid. I fear I cannot answer for him; but he will call as soon as he arrives, and apologize for himself."

Maltravers then hastily took his departure. He would not trust himself to do more than bow distantly to Evelyn; she looked at him reproachfully. So, then, it was really premeditated and resolved upon—his absence from the rectory; and why? She was grieved, she was offended—but more grieved than offended,—perhaps because esteem, interest, admiration, are more tolerant and charitable than love.

# CHAPTER VIII

> *Arethusa*. 'Tis well, my lord, your courting of ladies.
> *Claremont*. Sure this lady has a good turn done her against her will.
> PHILASTER.

In the breakfast-room at Knaresdean, the same day, and almost at the same hour, in which occurred the scene and conversation at the rectory recorded in our last chapter, sat Lord Vargrave and Caroline alone. The party had dispersed, as was usual, at noon. They heard at a distance the sounds of the billiard-balls. Lord Doltimore was playing with Colonel Legard, one of the best players in Europe, but who, fortunately for Doltimore, had of late made it a rule never to play for money. Mrs. and the Misses Cipher, and most of the guests, were in the billiard-room looking on. Lady Raby was writing letters, and Lord Raby riding over his home farm. Caroline and Lumley had been for some time in close and earnest conversation. Miss Merton was seated in a large armchair, much moved, with her handkerchief to her eyes. Lord Vargrave, with his back to the chimney-piece, was bending down and speaking in a very low voice, while his quick eye glanced, ever and anon, from the lady's countenance to the windows, to the doors, to be prepared against any interruption.

"No, my dear friend," said he, "believe me that I am sincere. My feelings for you are, indeed, such as no words can paint."

"Then why—"

"Why wish you wedded to another; why wed another myself? Caroline, I have often before explained to you that we are in this the victims of an inevitable fate. It is absolutely necessary that I should wed Miss Cameron. I never deceived you from the first. I should have loved her,—my heart would have accompanied my hand, but for your too seductive beauty, your superior mind!—yes, Caroline, your mind attracted me more than your beauty. Your mind seemed kindred to my own,—inspired with the proper and wise ambition which regards the fools of the world as puppets, as counters, as chessmen. For myself, a very angel from heaven could not make me give up the great game of life, yield to my enemies, slip from the ladder, unravel the web I have woven! Share my heart, my friendship, my schemes! this is the true and dignified affection that should exist between minds like ours; all the rest is the prejudice of children."

"Vargrave, I am ambitious, worldly: I own it; but I could give up all for you!"

"You think so, for you do not know the sacrifice. You see me now apparently rich, in power, courted; and this fate you are willing to share; and this fate you *should* share, were it the real one I could bestow on you. But reverse the medal. Deprived of office, fortune gone, debts pressing, destitution notorious, the ridicule of embarrassments, the disrepute attached to poverty and defeated ambition, an exile in some foreign town on the poor pension to which alone I should be entitled, a mendicant on the public purse; and that, too, so eaten into by demands and debts, that there is not a grocer in the next market-town who would envy the income of the retired minister! Retire, fallen, despised, in the prime of life, in the zenith of my hopes! Suppose that I could bear this for myself, could I bear it for you? *You*, born to be the ornament of courts! And you could you see me thus—life embittered, career lost—and feel, generous as you are, that your love had entailed on me, on us both, on our children, this miserable lot! Impossible, Caroline! we are too wise for such romance. It is not because we love too little, but because our love is worthy of each other, that we disdain to make love a curse! We cannot wrestle against the world, but we may shake hands with it, and worm the miser out of its treasures. My heart must be ever yours; my hand must be Miss Cameron's. Money I must have,—my whole career depends on it. It is literally with me the highwayman's choice,—money or life." Vargrave paused, and took Caroline's hand.

"I cannot reason with you," said she; "you know the strange empire you have obtained over me, and, certainly, in spite of all that has passed (and Caroline turned pale) I could bear anything rather than that you should hereafter reproach me for selfish disregard of your interests,—your just ambition."

"My noble friend! I do not say that I shall not feel a deep and sharp pang at seeing you wed another; but I shall be consoled by the thought that I have assisted to procure for you a station worthier of your merits than that which I can offer. Lord Doltimore is rich,—you will teach him to employ his riches well; he is weak,—your intellect will govern him; he is in love,—your beauty will suffice to preserve his regard. Ah, we shall be dear friends to the last!"

More—but to the same effect—did this able and crafty villain continue to address to Caroline, whom he alternately soothed, irritated, flattered, and revolted. Love him she certainly did, as far as love in her could extend; but perhaps his rank, his reputation, had served to win her affection; and; not knowing his embarrassments, she had encouraged a worldly hope that if Evelyn should reject his hand it might be offered to her. Under this impression she had trifled, she had coquetted, she had played with the serpent till it had coiled around her; and she could not escape its fascination and its folds. She was sincere,—she could have resigned much for Lord Vargrave; but his picture startled and appalled her. For difficulties in a palace she might be prepared; perhaps even for some privations in a *cottage ornee*,—but certainly not for penury in a lodging-house! She listened by degrees with more attention to Vargrave's description of the power and homage that would be hers if she could secure Lord Doltimore; she listened, and was in part consoled. But the thought of Evelyn again crossed her; and perhaps with natural jealousy was mingled some compunction at the fate to which Lord Vargrave thus coldly appeared to condemn one so lovely and so innocent.

"But do not, Vargrave," she said, "do not be too sanguine; Evelyn may reject you. She does not see you with my eyes; it is only a sense of honour that, as yet, forbids her openly to refuse the fulfilment of an engagement from which I know that she shrinks; and if she does refuse, and you be free,—and I another's—"

"Even in that case," interrupted Vargrave, "I must turn to the Golden Idol; my rank and name must buy me an heiress, if not so endowed as Evelyn, wealthy enough, at least, to take from my wheels the drag-chain of disreputable debt. But Evelyn—I will not doubt of her! her heart is still unoccupied!"

"True; as yet her affections are not engaged."

"And this Maltravers—she is romantic, I fancy—did he seem captivated by her beauty or her fortune?"

"No, indeed, I think not; he has been very little with us of late. He talked to her more as to a child,—there is a disparity of years."

"I am many years older than Maltravers," muttered Vargrave, moodily.

"You—but your *manner* is livelier, and, therefore, younger!"

"Fair flatterer! Maltravers does not love me: I fear his report of my character—"

"I never heard him speak of you, Vargrave; and I will do Evelyn the justice to say, that precisely as she does not love she esteems and respects you."

"Esteems! respects! these are the feelings for a prudent Hymen," said Vargrave, with a smile. "But, hark! I don't hear the billiard-balls; they may find us here,—we had better separate."

Lord Vargrave lounged into the billiard-room. The young men had just finished playing, and were about to visit Thunderer, who had won the race, and was now the property of Lord Doltimore.

Vargrave accompanied them to the stables; and after concealing his ignorance of horseflesh as well as he could, beneath a profusion of compliments on fore-hand, hind-quarters, breeding, bone, substance, and famous points, he contrived to draw Doltimore into the courtyard, while Colonel Legard remained in converse high with the head groom.

> "Doltimore, I leave Knaresdean to-morrow; you go to London, I suppose? Will you take a little packet for me to the Home Office?"

"Certainly, when I go; but I think of staying a few days with Legard's uncle—the old admiral; he has a hunting-box in the neighbourhood, and has asked us both over."

"Oh, I can detect the attraction; but certainly it is a fair one, the handsomest girl in the county; pity she has no money."

"I don't care for money," said Lord Doltimore, colouring, and settling his chin in his neckcloth; "but you are mistaken; I have no thoughts that way. Miss Merton is a very fine girl, but I doubt much if she cares for me. I would never marry any woman who was not very much in love with me." And Lord Doltimore laughed rather foolishly.

"You are more modest than clear-sighted," said Vargrave, smiling; "but mark my words,—I predict that the beauty of next season will be a certain Caroline Lady Doltimore."

The conversation dropped.

"I think that will be settled well," said Vargrave to himself, as he was dressing for dinner. "Caroline will manage Doltimore, and I shall manage one vote in the Lords and three in the Commons. I have already talked him into proper politics; a trifle all this, to be sure: but I had nothing else to amuse me, and one must never lose an occasion. Besides, Doltimore is rich, and rich friends are always useful. I have Caroline, too, in my power, and she may be of service with respect to this Evelyn, who, instead of loving, I half hate: she has crossed my path, robbed me of wealth; and now, if she does refuse me—but no, I will not think of *that*!"

# CHAPTER IX

OUT of our reach the gods have laid
Of time to come the event;
And laugh to see the fools afraid
Of what the knaves invent.—SEDLEY, *from Lycophron.*

THE next day Caroline returned to the rectory in Lady Raby's carria and two hours after her arrival came Lord Vargrave. Mr. Merton h secured the principal persons in the neighbourhood to meet a guest distinguished, and Lord Vargrave, bent on shining in the eyes of Evel charmed all with his affability and wit. Evelyn, he thought, seemed p and dispirited. He pertinaciously devoted himself to her all the eveni Her ripening understanding was better able than heretofore to appreci his abilities; yet, inwardly, she drew comparisons between his conversati and that of Maltravers, not to the advantage of the former. There was mu that amused but nothing that interested in Lord Vargrave's fluent ea When he attempted sentiment, the vein was hard and hollow; he was o at home on worldly topics. Caroline's spirits were, as usual in society, hi but her laugh seemed forced, and her eye absent.

The next day, after breakfast, Lord Vargrave walked alone to Burlei As he crossed the copse that bordered the park, a large Persian greyhou sprang towards him, barking loudly; and, lifting his eyes, he perceived form of a man walking slowly along one of the paths that intersected wood. He recognized Maltravers. They had not till then encountered si their meeting a few weeks before Florence's death; and a pang of conscie came across the schemer's cold heart. Years rolled away from the past; recalled the young, generous, ardent man, whom, ere the character or car of either had been developed, he had called his friend. He remembered th wild adventures and gay follies, in climes where they had been all in al each other; and the beardless boy, whose heart and purse were ever op to him, and to whose very errors of youth and inexperienced passion the elder and the wiser, had led and tempted, rose before him in cont to the grave and melancholy air of the battled and solitary man, who n slowly approached him,—the man whose proud career he had served thwart, whose heart his schemes had prematurely soured, whose best ye had been consumed in exile,—a sacrifice to the grave which a selfish dishonourable villany had prepared! Cesarini, the inmate of a mad-house, Florence in her shroud,—such were the visions the sight of Maltravers conjured up. And to the soul which the unwonted and momentary remorse awakened, a boding voice whispered, "And thinkest thou that thy schemes shall prosper, and thy aspirations succeed?" For the first time in his life, perhaps, the unimaginative Vargrave felt the mystery of a presentiment of warning and of evil.

The two men met, and with an emotion which seemed that of honest and real feeling, Lumley silently held out his hand, and half turned away his head.

"Lord Vargrave!" said Maltravers, with an equal agitation, "it is long since we have encountered."

"Long,—very long," answered Lumley, striving hard to regain his self-possession; "years have changed us both; but I trust it has still left in you, as it has in me, the remembrance of our old friendship."

Maltravers was silent, and Lord Vargrave continued,—

"You do not answer me, Maltravers. Can political differences, opposite pursuits, or the mere lapse of time, have sufficed to create an irrevocable gulf between us? Why may we not be friends again?"

"Friends!" echoed Maltravers; "at our age that word is not so lightly spoken, that tie is not so unthinkingly formed, as when we were younger men."

"But may not the old tie be renewed?"

"Our ways in life are different; and were I to scan your motives and career with the scrutinizing eyes of friendship, it might only serve to separate us yet more. I am sick of the great juggle of ambition, and I have no sympathy left for those who creep into the pint-bottle, or swallow the naked sword."

"If you despise the exhibition, why, then, let us laugh at it together, for I am as cynical as yourself."

"Ah," said Maltravers with a smile, half mournful, half bitter, "but are you not one of the Impostors?"

"Who ought better to judge of the Eleusiniana than one of the Initiated? But seriously, why on earth should political differences part private friendship? Thank Heaven! such has never been my maxim."

"If the differences be the result of honest convictions on either side,—no; but are you honest, Lumley?"

"Faith, I have got into the habit of thinking so; and habit's a second nature. However, I dare say we shall yet meet in the arena, so I must not betray my weak points. How is it, Maltravers, that they see so little of you at the rectory? You are a great favourite there. Have you any living that Charley Merton could hold with his own? You shake your head. And what think you of Miss Cameron, my intended?"

"You speak lightly. Perhaps you—"

> "Feel deeply,—you were going to say. I do. In the hand of my ward, Evelyn Cameron, I trust to obtain at once the domestic happiness to which I have as yet been a stranger, and the wealth necessary to my career."

Lord Vargrave continued, after a short pause, "Though my avocations have separated us so much, I have no doubt of her steady affection,—and, I may add, of her sense of honour. She alone can repair to me what else had been injustice in my uncle." He then proceeded to repeat the moral obligations which the late lord had imposed on Evelyn,—obligations that he greatly magnified. Maltravers listened attentively, and said little.

"And these obligations being fairly considered," added Vargrave, with a smile, "I think, even had I rivals, that they could scarcely in honour attempt to break an existing engagement."

"Not while the engagement lasted," answered Maltravers; "not till one or the other had declined to fulfil it, and therefore left both free: but I trust it will be an alliance in which all but affection will be forgotten; that of honour alone would be but a harsh tie."

"Assuredly," said Vargrave; and, as if satisfied with what had passed, he turned the conversation,—praised Burleigh, spoke of county matters, resumed his habitual gayety, though it was somewhat subdued, and promising to call again soon, he at last took his leave.

Maltravers pursued his solitary rambles, and his commune with himself was stern and searching.

"And so," thought he, "this prize is reserved for Vargrave! Why should I deem him unworthy of the treasure? May he not be worthier, at all events, than this soured temper and erring heart? And he is assured too of her affection! Why this jealous pang? Why can the fountain within never be exhausted? Why, through so many scenes and sufferings, have I still retained the vain madness of my youth,—the haunting susceptibility to love? This is my latest folly."